I held his warm paw and Mom's warm hand and counted
moon shadows on the ceiling till I fell asleep.

There was room for all of us on the couch bed. Dad blew out the candle and we lay close in the dark. Outside, the wind went *Woooooo* and the leaves went *Shiff, shiff* as they chased each other in the long grass.

"Don't worry about being scared," Mom told Biff. "Everyone's scared sometimes."

"Yeah, Biff," I said. "Don't worry about it at all."

Mom was behind Dad holding a candle.

"The wind knocked the lights off," she said. "And a tree branch was banging against our window. We decided to sleep down here on the couch."

"Biff thought you'd left us," I said. "He was so scared."

Mom stroked Biff's head. "Silly Biff! Don't you know we'd never leave you two guys?"

She stroked my head, too.

The dining room door burst open and a voice said: "Jake? Is that you?"

"Dad!" I ran and jumped up on him and Biff ran and jumped up, too.

"Hey!" Dad laughed. His arms closed around us. "I'm overflowing," he gasped.

I felt the scratchiness of his cheek and smelled his Dad smell. Biff's tail whipped against my legs.

"Waaa!" Biff was squirming to get below the table.

"Waaa!" The front part of the blob squirmed for the table too.

"Come back, Biff," I shouted.

And then I remembered the big mirror over the sideboard and I knew the horrible whiteness had been *me* carrying the blob that was Biff. That's all. So why was I standing here, howling too? Howling just as loudly as silly Biff?

A horrible whiteness seemed to be moving toward me out of the dark…a shapeless, blob-like whiteness.

Ghost's Hour! Spook's Hour!

"Help!" I yelled, dropping Biff in a heap and leaping backward against the table. Apples and oranges from the fruit bowl thudded past me to plop on the rug.

"Help!" The blob-like whiteness yelled, dropping the front part of itself and leaping back, too.

Through the long dining room windows I saw a smoky moon with clouds piled high against it. Our table seemed monstrously big. Chairs, hump-backed, clawed and crouched around it.

"Oooooooo," Biff moaned.

My heart gave a great jiggle.

I gathered him up, but he'd made himself heavy and he was hard to hold because of the shaking. Parts of him kept slipping as I carried him downstairs.

Tick, tick, went the big clock.

Swiiiish, swiiiish, went the pendulum.

Clatter, rattle, shuffle, shiff went the dead leaves against the house.

"Twelve o'clock. Midnight," I said. And I thought, Ghost's Hour, Spook's Hour. But I didn't tell Biff.

He threw himself across my feet, warm and trembly. In a way I wanted to stay here, too, or run back to bed and pull the blankets over my head. But here was too scary and back there would be scarier still.

"Come, Biff," I said.

He wouldn't.

We stood at the top of the stairs with the dark pushing against us.

"Mom? Dad?" My voice disappeared into the dark cave below.

The dining room clock went:

BOOM
BOOM
BOOM
BOOM
BOOM
BOOM
BOOM
BOOM
BOOM
BOOM
BOOM
BOOM

Something went *Craaak* against the window. *Craak, slither, whiiish*! Something was out there. Black, snaky things pounced on the glass.

I tried to get behind Biff but he was trying to get behind me. I made myself peer over his back.

"Whew!" I said, standing up and uncurling my fingers from Biff's fur. "It's only our black, snaky tree branches, silly Biff. You don't have to be *this* scared. Let's go find Mom and Dad."

We padded fast along the hallway to my parents' room.

"Mom?" I whispered. "Dad?"

No one answered.

I clicked the lightswitch. No light again.

Woooooo went the wind. *Woooooo.*

I shuffled across to the bed and felt around. The sheets were warm and lumpy but the bed was empty. Where were Mom and Dad?

"Ooooooo," Biff howled.

"Quit that," I said, though I wanted to howl myself. Where could they be?

I pushed it again.

Nothing happened again.

"Oh, oh, Biff," I whispered. "I don't like this. Let's get out of here."

My bedroom door moaned when I opened it.

Eeeeeee.

"Eeeeeee," Biff moaned.

"It's OK," I said. "I think this door always creaks. I think it sounds louder at night." It was good to have Biff to talk to.

An icy wetness touched my toes and I leaped back. "Eek! What…?"

Then I remembered Biff, my big white dog who sleeps under my bed at night. Biff has the coldest, wettest nose.

"Hi, Biff," I said. I felt for the bedside lamp and pushed the button.

Nothing happened.

When I woke up it was really dark.
Something went *Woooooo* outside my
window.

"Don't be scared," I told myself. "It's just
the wind." I slid out of bed.

For my cousin, Joan Anderson Geating.
—E.B.

Clarion Books
Ticknor & Fields, a Houghton Mifflin Company
Text copyright © 1987 by Eve Bunting
Illustrations copyright © 1987 by Donald Carrick

Library of Congress Cataloging-in-Publication Data
Bunting, Eve, 1928–
      Ghost's hour, spook's hour.
      Summary: Scary incidents at midnight give Biff
the dog and his master a frightening time but all
turn out to have good explanations.
      [1. Night—Fiction.   2. Fear—Fiction.
3. Dogs—Fiction]   I. Carrick, Donald, ill.
II. Title.
PZ7.B91527Ghhi   1987   [E]   86-31674
ISBN 0-89919-484-2

NI 10 9 8 7 6 5 4 3

Ghost's Hour,
Spook's Hour

by Eve Bunting
Illustrated by Donald Carrick

Clarion Books
TICKNOR & FIELDS : A HOUGHTON MIFFLIN COMPANY
New York